Alex

Alex

Ayesha Baig

Library of Congress Control Number:		2019904154
ISBN:	Hardcover	978-1-7960-2626-9
	Softcover	978-1-7960-2625-2
	eBook	978-1-7960-2624-5

Print information available on the last page.

Rev. date: 04/10/2019

To order additional copies of this book, contact:
Xlibris
1-888-795-4274
www.Xlibris.com
Orders@Xlibris.com
795270

It was a small room that contained a bed and clutter throughout. A ceiling fan hung over the bed to provide the smallest amount of ventilation yet the biggest amount of noise. The walls were covered with art, posters, and his original masterpieces. The one small window in the room was covered in dirt and never opened. The floor was barely visible under the clothing, newspapers, sketchpads, and leftover to go boxes.

Have you ever felt loved? Truly loved by another person. The feeling that you are wanted by someone. The feeling that you are important. That little feeling that makes all the difference. Kinda makes life worth living, doesn't it?

He lay on his bed creating a new world within his world. Not one confined by the walls, the door, the window, or his bed, but one that was his own. He is the owner and the servant. He gazed up at the ceiling and it surrounded him, took over him and he no longer is in one world, but two worlds at the same time.

> He is 5 years old, sitting on the couch, quietly waiting. Waiting for the storm to come through the door. Waiting for the break in the silence. Waiting for Her. As usual, she bangs open the door, stumbles in, and slams the door shut. A new man with her again. She stutters "Hi Baby!" with her magical smile that could give as fast as it could take. A bottle in one hand and a bud in the other. She looked to the man and said, "That's my

son." She points to him. He wanted her, so badly, to tell the man to go way, but instead she walked him to her room and shut the door. He sat in silence once again. For how long, he doesn't remember, but it was morning.

The alarm went off and he sat up in bed. Another morning, another day, another opportunity. As he got dressed he looked at the mirror to brush his hair. There wasn't a point, but he did anyway. He saw to the side the picture he had put up of a man with a trophy. Dressed in an expensive tuxedo with the brightest smile holding a gold trophy that glittered in the light.

"And the award goes to Mr. Alexander Holloway." Everyone begins to applaud. People are standing up to greet him and give him well wishes. He walks up to the stage and holds his trophy. "Alex please say a few words for all your fans out there." Says the announcer. "Well, I guess I could share a few words. First of all, I would like to thank all my fans, for allowing me this opportunity to achieve such success and accolades. Also everyone that has supported me throughout my life to help me make this wonderful journey, we call Life. Also thank you to everyone here, for thinking I'm capable of this reward. Thank you everyone." He walks off stage, as people come towards him with hugs, handshakes, and smiles.

Bam! He heard the frame drop to the floor. He picked it up and put It back on the shelf. He finished getting reading and started the walk to work. The day was sunny with a few skinny clouds scattered around the sun. he walked down the street when he crossed the ice cream shop and saw a mother with her child. The boy enjoying his ice cream cone a little too much and getting it all over his mouth as his mother watched with amusement and wiping his face whenever she got a chance.

"Sit straight Alex!" his mother shouted at him. "If you can't sit than stand in the corner." She took his cup from him and threw it in the sink. "Look what you have done! It's such a mess now! Here clean it up!" she walked over to the counter and lit her cigarette watching him wipe up the milk he spilt on the floor. As she looked for something to drink and began slamming the counter doors.

Honk Honk!! "Hey buddy! Watch where you are walking!" He stepped over to the curb and continued the walk. As he entered the main building the other guys from work laughed at him. As usual they came towards him with clear intention to try and mock him again today.

"Hey Alex! Back to Work again?!" the big guy said as he tried to put his arm around Alex trying to get a grip on him.

"Yea" he moved the guy's hand and tried to walk ahead when the short guy came up.

"Are you mad Alex? How come you never talk to us? We want to be your friends too!" the whole group began to laugh as if it was the funniest thing they heard all day.

****

The production office was like any other office. It was divided so that different aspects of production were on each floor of the building. As the production assistant, Nisha worked on the top floor for Kelly Summers. Kelly was the production manager and a perfectionist in every sense. Nisha didn't mind Kelly because she knew that Kelly had a lot of connections in the industry and knew the ins and outs of the business.

Nisha had to be in the office before 9 am sharp, because Kelly was always on time. Usually Nisha came at 8 to catch up on all the errands she knew she would have to do for Kelly. Today, however, she was late. As she entered the building she sorted her files. She knew she had to have all the files ready for Kelly before she got to the office.

The main lobby was always crowded in the morning as people began to check in for work. She headed towards the elevators when she noticed a group of the stagehands gathered around the elevators waiting.

They were laughing at something. She looked back at the file on top, the progress report for last month. She had to keep that on top, Kelly would most likely ask for that first. She heard the laughter of the group get louder as she approached them. She checked the files again. Before she could look up to check her distance someone jabbed her shoulder and she dropped all the files. She looked up stunned and angry. The group of men hushed and walked away, except for one. He bent down and started to pick up the papers. She got down next to him and picked up the rest of the files. She only had 15 minutes to get up to the office and fix the mess of files. She quickly took the papers from him, said thank you, and walked into the open elevator.

****

"I'm heading out for lunch. I will be back at 1." Kelly said to Nisha as she headed out the door.

"Okay, will see you at 1 Ms. Summers." Nisha sat at her desk, finishing up the emails to directors. She had a cup of coffee and a muffin for breakfast. After the elevator incident, she had panicked to get all the files in order and on Kelly Summers desk before 9. Now she was ready for lunch. She clicked send on the email and grabbed her bag. The building had one cafeteria off the lobby. The food wasn't bad, but wasn't the best either. It was already 12:15, so she opted to see what the cafeteria had today.

"No. No. No." She mumbled to herself. Finally towards the end she found the last salad. She paid the lady and was headed out the door. As she walked by the patio she saw him scribbling on some paper.

She went to the table, "Is this seat taken?" she sat down with waiting for an answer. He closed his journal.

"No." he looked at her in confusion.

"I'm sorry. I didn't mean to startle you. I just saw you sitting alone, so I came to say thank you."

He picked at the torn edges of his journal.

She continued, "Thank you. Um. Okay than I will leave you alone, uh what did you say your name was?"

"I didn't"

"oh. Well you can tell me now" she smiled as she waited for his answer.

"Alex." He looked at his journal.

"It was nice to meet you Alex. I have to get back." She pointed towards the building, "Bye." She walked back to the office.

****

"Good morning Ms. Summers" She stood up from her desk to greet her boss as she walked through the office doors.

"I need to see you in my office." She walked into her office and Nisha walked behind her carry a notepad.

"We have a complication in the lighting department. The stagehands have completed the set, but the stage director, Ron, says there is some wiring difficulty. I want you to go down to the set and find out what the problem is and figure out the solution first thing today. Don't come back until it is finish. I have a meeting in 20 minutes and I need to leave. Call my appointments for later today and confirm all of them. Also I need the costume directors to give me updates on the designs, make sure you get them today. I want my salad for lunch at 11:30, I have meeting at 12:15. And tell the person who is in charge of cleaning my office if they put the trash can on the right side of my desk again they can find another office to clean. That's it." She looked at Nisha for the first time all morning.

"No ma'am. I'll get to the lighting first."

"Alright. Where is the budget report?"

"I put it on your desk right there on the tray." Nisha nodded towards the back wall of the office. Kelly turned and stood staring into the file. Then she waved to Nisha as she sat at her computer. Nisha shut the door, and walked to her desk to look up which sets were still under construction. Once she noted down the location of the set, she walked back to Kelly's office.

"I'm going to the set, just letting you know I won't be at my desk, but I have my phone with me if you need anything."

"Fine." Kelly continued to type on her computer.

Nisha shut the door and headed towards the elevator. She walked out of the main office building and across the lot to the sets. There were 4 different sets, but the particular one in question was farthest from the office.

She walked into what looked like an auditorium. It was pitch black, the only lighting being the door she came through.

"Hello?!" she shouted into darkness trying to walk across the stage without tripping on her shoes. "Is there anyone in here?" She was almost to the center of the stage stepping slowly toward the other end. "I'm from the production office, Kelly Summers sent me to check with Ron." Apparently no one was here, but she continued to walk toward the red exit light on the other side. She had her clipboard incase she needed to write anything and she gripped it tightly to her chest as she slowly stepped forward. It was when she was reaching the end of the stage that the lights begin to sparkle all around her. She froze in her spot a little blinded and a little amazed. It looked as if she was really outside looking up at a mountain with millions of stars sparkling overhead. She looked behind her and the stage was lit up as well. She walked around the stage and absorbed the amazing pergola that stood in the middle of the ground. It was in the midst of her observation that she heard the other door open. A man walked through the door and halted when he saw her.

"Hi. I'm Nisha from the production office. Kelly Summers sent me to check the lighting problem. Which I guess is solved" She walked towards the man as he walked towards her and then stopped to put something down.

"Yea everything is fine." He responded. She recognized the man but couldn't remember from where.

"Okay, so who fixed it?"

"I did." He stepped into the light of the stage, "It was a light thing."

"Hey I know you!" she realized it was him from a few days ago. What was his name, she thought to herself. "Well this place looks beautiful! I have never seen any of the sets, but this is just amazing!"

"Yea the pergola took me a while."

"You did that? By yourself?" clearly the look on her face was astonishment because he smiled looking down at the floor.

He moved his hair back, "Yea."

"Wow. Uh I'm sorry what was your name?"

"Alex"

"Alex! Yes that's it! Alex you did a great job!"

"Thanks"

"Okay. I have to go and finish the rest of my errands. Nice seeing you again Alex!" She turned around and walked out from the same door she came in and waved to Alex. He was looking at the pergola.

****

"Nisha!" Raj came walking towards her. He was dressed in his usual suit and tie, always ready for business. He was tall and handsome. He had this charm about him that made anyone feel appreciated. She had known Raj since she was 2. They went to the same pre-school, private school, and university. They knew everything about each other. Their parents had been good friends since India, and still met on a regular basis.

"So, are you ready to go?" he asked her as he gave her a hug.

"Yeah. I'm so hungry!" they headed towards the car.

As Raj started the car Nisha's phone rang.

"Hello." She spoke quietly, "No. with Raj. No. I don't want to Ma." Raj looked at Nisha as she rolled her eyes at the windshield. She handed him the phone. Her mom was on the other side.

"Raj come over to our place for lunch. Pooja is here and we want to have a family lunch. Convince Nisha please." She spoke without giving him a chance, a habit she shared with her daughter.

"Okay. We will be there soon." He hung up and handed the phone back to Nisha.

"I don't know why you always agree with her. We are supposed to be going out for lunch."

"I will take you out for dinner. Just don't get upset."

When they got to the house, Pooja was already setting the table for everyone while Nisha's parents sat at the table. Her mom giving instructions between conversations with her dad, "Pooja get the forks also." She glanced around the table and noticed Raj. "Raj you came!" She stood up and walked over toward them. "Nisha meri bachi." She hugged her daughter and walked with them to the table.

Her father sat at the end of the table. To his right was her mother's empty chair. He motioned for Raj to take the seat on his left as Pooja was taking her seat next to her mom. Nisha walked to her dad and gave him a hug then sat next to Raj.

"How is everything Raj?" Pooja asked once they were all seated.

"Everything is good. How about you?"

Nisha was busy grabbing a dish in front of Raj, which was obviously too heavy for her so he held it for her while she scooped rice onto her plate. "Thanks" she whispered as Pooja continued

"Just very busy at work. I haven't seen you in a while." She passed a round dish to her mother, who helped herself and put some in her husband's plate as well.

"Would you like some Raj?"

"No aunty. Nisha how about you?"

"No. It's too fattening." She continued to eat without looking up.

"Nisha eat slowly, what's the hurry?!" her mother said as she put the dish down on the table.

"I'm in a hurry. I have to get back to work. My lunch break is only an hour." She took another bite of food.

"I don't get why you are working there when you can do something better. This dream of yours is turning into a nightmare." Nisha glared at her mother. She picked up her glass of water and drank it down in a gulp.

"I never asked for your opinion." She said flatly.

"What do you mean? Look at you. You work at this place and haven't gotten any acting jobs. It's a waste of time. Look at Pooja. She is a successful doctor. Why didn't you do medicine like her? You could have your life set like her."

Nisha dropped her fork on her plate. "I don't want to be Pooja. It you can't support me its fine. I don't need it, but this is what I want and I don't care what you think!"

"Nisha, is this how you talk to your mother?"

"I'm done. Let's go Raj." She stood from the table, put her napkin by the plate, and walked out without saying anything else. Raj was stunned by what taken place. He looked across the table at Pooja with bewilderment. She nodded at him and he knew what that meant. He stood, "Thank you so much for the lunch, it was great. I'll meet you all next time." He walked out and they heard the beep of the alarm signaling he had left.

Pooja turned to her mother, "Why do you say things like that to her? Just leave her alone. If that is what she wants let her do it. Her mother sat in silence staring at her plate.

"Gayatri, tumhe aise nahi bolna chahiye tha. I agree with Pooja." Her dad put his hand on her moms. She raised her hands out from under his.

"Kya nahi bolna chahiye tha? Uska dimagh kharab hogaya hai! Aapne bigaar ke rakhdiya hai ussay!" She stood up and took her plate to the kitchen throwing it in the sink and walking out.

Pooja and her dad just stared at each other as her mom left. Pooja finished her food and said goodbye to her father.

****

"Good Morning Ms. Summers." Nisha handed Kelly a file as she walked passed her, as usual.

"Good Morning Nisha." She flipped through the list after list of names of stagehands that were working part time for the production company. She waved for Nisha to follow her into her office.

"Yes?" Nisha stood in her regular spot in front of Kelly's desk with her notepad.

"Most of our sets on the lot are complete. Besides the two Ron mentioned. It will be a waste to continue to have so many people on the payroll, so I need you to start typing up their notifications, and make sure they all receive their last paycheck." She continued to scan the pages.

"Let's see, from this list Ron wanted to keep only 10 stagehands. This was the Mountain set, so I presume they were good at what they did. The following people need to be notified," she paused and began to read the list, "Robert, Stuart, Matthew, Steven, Alexander…"

"Alexander?" Nisha stopped to look at her boss.

"Yes. Alexander."

"If you don't mind, uh I would like to say something."

Kelly stared at her assistant in puzzlement, "Go ahead."

"I don't think you should fire Alex…I mean Alexander."

"Why is that? A friend of yours?"

"No. No. I saw his work. It was incredible. Do you remember the lighting problem from the other day? He had already fixed it when I got there. He did it all alone. He even made the pergola. I think it would be a loss for the company, that's all." She looked back at her notepad.

"Alright, don't put his name on the list. I will talk to Ron about your friend Alex. Shall we continue?"

"Yes Ms. Summers."

Kelly began to list off the remaining names that were to be notified.

****

He waited outside of the home. It had been 20 minutes since he had arrived, but didn't know how to go inside. The people were arriving one after another. He shouldn't have come here, except Nisha had insisted on him coming. He looked up and saw a black car stop in the driveway in front of the house.

> He opened the door and stepped out of the car, he went to the other side to open the door for Nisha. He stood in front of the car door for a minute and adjusted his tuxedo and tie, than opened the door. As she stepped out he couldn't help but stare at her. She smiled at him and put her arms around his, she whispered "stop acting

like this is the first time you have seen me." It did feel
like the first time and she looked stunning.

"Hey." She looked at him with curiosity in her eyes. "How long
have you been standing here? I've been waiting for you. It's as if the
praising ceremony for my sister and Raj is never ending." He turned
back towards the driveway; the couple had now arrived at the door and
was going inside. "Alex. I'm talking to you; can you at least pretend to
pay attention?" He looked at her, she was beautiful. "Yea, I think I'm
gonna go."

"What?! Why?! You just got here! You are not going anywhere,
come inside with me and give me company. I can't take these people
anymore." She grabbed his hand and pulled him through the door into
the house. There were so many people in the home. She kept a tight grip
on his hand and guided him through the people. Finally she stopped
in front of an older man with graying hair and alittle balding at the top
of his head. He was dressed like all the other men in a suit. Holding a
glass of champagne he smiled at Nisha, "Daddy, this is my friend from
work. Alex." Her father smiled and nodded his head "Hello Mr. Alex.
Nisha has told me many good things about you." Alex shook his hand
"Hello sir". As soon as he let go, Nisha was already pulling him toward
another crowd of people.

"Mother and di, this is Alex. The guy from work" the women, one
dressed like Nisha in a dress and the other in some sort of wrapping,
just looked him up and down and stared. "Hi bolo maa, aise ghoor ke
mat dekho"

Nisha's mother, the one dressed in the different outfit put her hand
out for him, "Hi Alex, nice to meet you."

He took her hand "Nice to meet you" she smiled at him and the
resemblance was astonishing, Nisha's mother had the same magical
smile as her daughter.

"Well you must excuse me there are so many other guests to greet.
Enjoy." And she walked away taking Nisha's sister with her.

"Ignore those two" Nisha said as they left. "My mother will never
change she only cares for one and one only. My sister. You know when

we were little it was always Nisha why can't you be like Priya. Priya is so sweet, so smart, so cultured. I don't give a damn. I don't want to be Priya, I want to be Nisha." Raj put his arm around her waist. She flinched, and tried to move from him.

"Hey Alex, what are you doing here? I didn't think guys like you came to these things." He smiled at Alex.

"Hey Raj. Nisha asked me to come." Raj looked at Nisha, "is that so? I didn't know about this Nisha."

She got away from his grip, "Yea I asked him, is that a problem? I can't invite guests to my own home?"

Finally, he was able to convince Nisha to let him go home. This gathering had been more than enough for him. She had insisted on walking him out, even though Raj wasn't too happy about it.

The moon was full and bright. The quietness was a relief from all the noise, and all he could here was the wind through the trees. Nisha followed behind him.

"It's such a beautiful night, isn't it?" he nodded. "By the way Alex, I wanted to thank you for coming tonight. I kinda thought you wouldn't come. You know since you don't like big crowds and people." She turned towards him.

"It's no big deal, Nisha." They stood quietly looking up at the sky and the stars. He looked at her one more time in the moonlight before he left. She was just as amazing in this light as any other. All of a sudden, she looked at him. Her big brown eyes were captivating and her smile made him freeze in his spot. "I should go. It's late."

"Alright, take care Alex." She leaned into him and kissed him on the cheek, "thanks once again" she whispered in his ear. He could barely whisper the words "You're welcome" she stepped back and watched as he began his walk home.

****

"Alex! Alex!!"

He turned around to see Nisha running towards him. "What the Hell! I've been yelling your name for so long!! Why aren't you stopping?"

"Sorry. I didn't hear you. I was thinking about something."

"Yea, whatever. Hey what are you doing tonight? Would you like to come to dinner with me and Raj?"

"No. I'm busy."

"Hmm, you are? Doing what?"

"Stuff. You go and have fun."

"No, I was only going to dinner if you were going to go. I don't want to have fun with Raj. You know what? How about we just go for dinner?"

"Nisha, I'm busy." She gave him her pouty look. "Please Alex Please!" she pulled his arm, "Don't make me suffer with Raj. Please! I'm begging you." She smiled and winked at him,

"Fine, where would you like to go?"

"YaY! Meet me at 6! At my place!" She kissed his cheek and went to her car. An official date with Nisha, he was concerned. What if Raj found out about this? He would not be happy. He should have said no.

It was 6 pm; she had called earlier and asked for him to come to the restaurant instead of her house. He walked into the restaurant and saw her at the table. She looked up and waved for him to come to the table. He went to the table and sat down, "Hi" she smiled at him.

"Hey. How are you?" He was uncomfortable with all these people sitting so close to them.

"I'm doing just fine. Thank you so much for coming for me. You have no idea how happy this makes me, not having to deal with Raj and his boring business talks again tonight." She giggled and reached out and touched his hand. "Have you been here before?"

"Huh? No." he looked around at the tables near their table. This is too many people watching him.

"Well they have the best food. Trust me, my family comes her all the time. I hope you didn't mind me asking you to come here instead of the house. My mother was having an emotional breakdown today.

I didn't want you to see the crazy side of my family, yet." She laughed, her laughter was contagious. He had to laugh as well.

"Oh My God! Alex you actually laugh too? I'm amazed!" they both laughed for a bit until the waiter interrupted them.

"what can I get you?" Nisha looked up at him," I would like to have the salad please, and Alex what about you?" She handed him the menu.

Everything was way over his budget, but he had to eat. "I don't know how about the sandwhich."

"anything to drink with that?' the waiter looked more irritated than they did.

"No thanks I will just have water." She looked to Alex and he nodded in agreement, "make that two waters." The waiter took the menu and walked away with the least interest in their order or them.

As they waited for their order Alex began to get fidgcty. The tables were so close. He tried to stay calm. A group of kids cam in and sat next to their table creatimg more noise and less distance between thme. Alex could feel them right behind him. He became more anxious. He started to tap on the table at first subtle, then slowly faster.

Nisha looked at the crowd that came in today. She watchd Alex and noiced he was quiet as usual bua little anxious, "So Alex, how was work today?" She was trying to divert his attention towards her.

"Huh?" He looked at her. He tried to focus all his attention on her, "it was fine"

"Oh well…that's good"

"Nisha I'm sorry but can we go out?"

"We are Out"

"No. let's get out from here. I will take you somewhere else." He started to fidget.

"Okay. That's fine with me. Let's go."

They got up and walked out of the restaurant. The fresh air calmed Alex a little and he relaxed. "Nisha I'm sorry about that" he pointed towards the restaurant. "But don't worry I will buy you dinner in exchange."

"I'm glad you feel better. It was crowded in there." They continued to walk along the sidewalk.

"so how did it happen?" he asked her.

"What happened?"

"how did a guy like Raj get someone like you?"

"what?" she looked confused.

"I mean, you are pretty and he's not."

"well it didn't happen. He thinks it did, but I don't think of him like that. I just can't say no. anyways let's go back to the pretty thing. What was that?"

"It's true. You are too pretty for him."

"And...?"

"and what?"

"Keep going, I think this is the first time you are complimenting me"

"Well I know when you come to work you are always late, because you sit and think in your car. Even though you don't like Raj you bring him coffee every morning. You want to be an actress, but you don't want to disappoint your parents."

"Wow! How do you know all this?!"

"I just do." He shrugged his shoulders.

"It's creepy. So what about you? What do you want?"

"Happiness"

"simple. Nice answer. How about your parents?"

"don't have anyone."

"Hmm. That must be nice. No one to question you or give answers to."

"sometimes"

"where do you live?"

"in an apartment"

"Girlfriends?"

"nope"

"Are you always so quiet?"

"Do you always ask so many questions?"

"No! but you don't talk, so I'm asking."

"Okay let me ask you something."

"Sure"

"Why is Raj not your boyfriend, but you are his girlfriend?"

"That's because he asked to go out and I said yes and thought we were dating, which we aren't."

"What do your parents think?

"About what?"

"Raj"

"Nothing. They like him."

"What do they think about me?"

"Nothing. They like you too."

"They do?"

"Yea."

"Hard to believe since they always seem upset when they see me."

"Do they?"

Alex pointed towards a small café. "lets go in here. Its nice and quiet"

They sat in the corner table waiting for the waiters. The sky was getting dark and streetlights came on down the lane. A waiter came up to their table and handed them a menu, "what can I get for you?"

"I will have the sandwich" Alex answered first. "I will have the salad. Thank you" ordered Nisha.

After dinner they had coffee and he walked her back to her car at the end of the street.

"thanks for making me come. I don't usually like to eat out."

"No problem. I'm glad you came. I hope you had fun." She smiled as they got closer to the car.

"I did. You are interesting."

"Am I?"

"yea. There is more to you than you lead on."

"I guess." she got her keys out as she came to her car. "do you want a ride?"

"no. I live couple of blocks from here, and it is late you should get home."

"Okay. Good night Alex." She got in her car and drove home. He watched her drive away and started walking home.

****

"Yeah. Okay. Ahaan, I get it. Yeah. Okay MOM! I get it I told you I will give her the file on the way home. Okay I will talk to you later. Bye." She hung up the phone and walked to her car. Another day of work had ended at the production company. Nisha still hadn't gotten any news from any of the auditions. She started the car and began to drive out of the parking lot. As she drove towards the exit, she saw Alex walking alone on the road. She honked the horn and rolled down the window as she got closer to him.

"Hey! Need a Ride?" Alex stopped in his footstep, looked up to see Nisha in the car.

"No, I'm alright. Thanks." He started to walk but she honked again. "listen, just get in the car and don't make me beg." She motioned with her eyes for him to get in the car. He opened the door and sat down next to her. "you don't have to do this, you know" he shut the door and she drove forward. They sat in silence for a while. "I hope you don't mind, but I have to drop some files off to my sister at the hospital. It shouldn't take too long. Is that okay?" she looked to him and than back at the road, "Yea that is fine. I don't have anywhere to be right now. You didn't have to give me a ride if you are busy." She didn't respond to his comment. He sat quietly while she drove to the hospital.

They walked up the steps to the second floor of the hospital to the private offices. As they walked down the corridor, Nisha stopped in front of a door <u>Dr. Pooja Kapoor.</u> this was Nisha's sister's office. She opened the door and walked in.

"Excuse me Doctor, if you don't mind can I come in?" Pooja looked up from her files. "No, leave. I don't have time for psychos like you right now." "Ha. Ha. Ha. You are so funny. Does that come with the job?" Nisha walked right into the office and touched the souvenirs on Pooja's desk.

"Stop touching everything. You know this is not an acting class right? I actually work here. What do you want?" pooja hit Nisha's hand with her pen. "Seriously do you have to touch everything on my desk? You are moving everything." Nisha made a face at her sister. "God! You are so annoying Pooja. So boring. Is this why Arjun doesn't visit you at work? Cause you treat him like a patient? Or aheemm does he get the special treatment?" Nisha winked at Pooja. Pooja glared at her sister. "Alex, what are you doing with this good for nothing brat?" She stood up and shook his hand. "oh nothing, she insisted on taking me home." Pooja raised her eyebrows at Nisha. "Oh I see." She walked around the desk toward her sister. "So why are you here again?" Nisha handed her the files in her hand. "Mom said to give these to you. You left them at home this morning." She handed pooja the files and walked toward a bright board. "Who's x-rays are these?" she turned to look at her sister. "Obviously not yours. They are patients of mine." Pooja stood and read the files while Nisha continued to stare at the board.

Alex walked over next to her and looked at them. "wow these are pretty interesting, Pooja." Pooja walked over to the X-ray board. "Yea, you see the brain is so compact. These scans tell us a lot about the problems in the patient. See this first scan," she pointed to the scan on the far left. "this is a patient that is suffering from a brain tumor. You see the spot right here." She pointed to a white spot on the scan. "blah blah blah. My god Pooja who cares what they are suffering from. Think of the people they are. How their lives are. We all know about the scans and all, but what about the personality behind them?" Nisha was apparently bored from the conversation. Pooja was irritated by her sister's lack of interest, "OH really Nisha? What do you see in the X-rays?" Nisha looked hard at the scans, "You know what I see Alex?"

"What?"

"Well, see here. This patient seems to be very smart. Look at the size of the brain!" she pointed at the x-ray to the far right of the board. He stared into the board. "can you stop staring at my brain please sir?" Alex was astonished he stepped back in shock and turned around. Standing in the corner of the office by the bookshelf was a man dressed in a blue suit and a hat.

"He must have been a lawyer, don't you think Alex?" Nisha looked to Alex for a response; instead he was staring back at the bookcase. "Alex?" She nudged him with her elbow.

"Y-e-aa?"

"I asked what you think his profession was. You aren't listening again."

"He was a detective Nisha. A good one."

"How do you know that?" she wasn't sure what he was looking at so she stood in front of him.

"Oh. I am guessing like you." He walked out of the room.

"I guess I should go. See you at home Di." She ran out the office after Alex.

****

"So you're not going to show me your place?" Nisha said as Alex was getting out of her car. "My place is really nothing and well actually its dirty." Alex said looking at her, he wasn't so sure if she would like his place. Maybe it wasn't a big deal if she came inside for a bit he thought.

"OH! So this is your apartment? Pretty fancy" Nisha said in a sarcastic tone as she tried finding a place to sit. Alex looked around nervously started picking up his shirts and dirty socks off the floor. "Yea this is my place; sorry I haven't had any time to clean it"

"It's okay! Let me help you clean this place up a bit" As Nisha wandered around picking up clothes here and there and putting them on the dresser. Alex watched her in awe as she gracefully walked around in his apartment with no hesitation at all. He wondered if she could belong here with him.

Nisha turned towards him "hello Alex?!? Is anyone there? What are you doing!?"

"Oh sorry"

"Alex you sometimes really worry me." she picked up his clothes, text books, and old soda cans near his bedroom.

"Why are you worried?" Alex walked towards her.

"Well I always catch you day dreaming and not listening to me when I'm talking to you."

He walked closer to her and took the stuff from her hand. "I'm sorry, sometimes I get lost in my own thoughts."

Nisha grabbed his hand "Alex, You are one of a kind" She walked up really close to him and kissed him. "Nisha you are one of a kind too" he backed up and threw the items on the table near his bed.

"Is something wrong Alex?" Nisha asked as he turned back around.

"No, nothing is wrong." He walked back towards the couch.

"Why is it that every time I try to get close to you, you back away like you don't want to be close to me. I thought you liked me more?" she walked up behind him.

He looked at Her beautiful face, her perfect body, the long dark hair, and the big brown eyes. "It's not that Nisha. I don't want to do anything to you that will get you in trouble. You have everything going for you and I don't want to mess it up."

"Mess it up? How can you mess it up? You aren't getting me in trouble or messing it up. You are what I want now. Can't you see I want you!" He kissed her before she could say anything else. He continued to kiss her, her lips pressed against his; he just wanted more of her. Somehow he couldn't stop himself this time. He put his arms around her, pulled her to his body, and lifted her up. He carried her to his bed.

When he opened his eyes she was asleep, her breathing calm and steady. She had her arm across his chest and her head on his right arm. He could smell the fresh perfume scent in her hair. The bed sheet covered her body, but he could see the mark on her shoulder blade. He touched the mark. She was warm. He remembered what had happened the night before. It still felt like a fantasy, but here she was in his bed, safe and asleep. He felt her move and she looked up at him. She gazed into his eyes, as if knowing what he was thinking; she smiled and hugged him tightly,

"I'm glad you are up. I have to get ready for work and so do you." he started to get out of bed but she tightened her grip around him. He didn't understand and she whispered, "Let's take the day off."

"why?"

"I like it right here and I don't want it to end." She put her head on the pillow as she continued to smile at him.

"I can't"

"Why?"

"Nisha, I have to work"

"But why? You don't like my company?"

"I love you and I love your company, but I work."

"Please?" she pouted as she grabbed his hand.

"Fine. What are we going to do?"

"I think you already know."

"Can we eat first? I'm hungry" he grabbed his shirt from the floor by the bed and went to the kitchen.

She picked up her phone to check the missed calls and texts.

RAJ: NISHA WHERE ARE YOU?

POOJA: IT'S 12:35 I CALLED YOU AND RAJ WHERE ARE YOU GUYS? CALL ME WHEN YOU GET THIS.

RAJ: CALL ME.

RAJ: IT'S BEEN ALL NIGHT WHAT'S WRONG?

She called Pooja right away, "Hey Di."

"Where are you? I've been worried. You were supposed to have dinner with us."

"Yea, I'm sorry I had some stuff to take care of."

"What stuff?"

"Nothing really. Just helping Alex with his apartment"

"Okay, are you still there?"

"Yea. Please don't tell Raj anything. I still haven't talked to him."

"Hmm. Well I have to go see a patient. Bye"

She hung up the phone and listened to Alex move around the kitchen. He appeared at the door a few minutes later.

"I don't have much, but you like toast?"

"Um, yea."

He put the tray on the bed next to her and grabbed a piece of toast off the plate and handed to her. Then he took another piece and began to eat it. They ate quietly and Nisha noticed the walls in the light. Color was splashed all over the wall across the bed.

"Wow." she mumbled.

She wrapped the bed sheet around her as she got out of bed and walked over to the wall. she touched the paint and ran her hand across the wall. she looked over her shoulders, "Did you do this?"

"Yea"

"It's amazing! I've never seen anything like this."

****

They walked into the front door of Nisha's house. He could hear the laughter from the other room, and he stopped in the foyer. "Nisha, I can't do this. It's just not me." Nisha turned around and pressed his arm. She came up close to him, "Please Alex. This means a lot to me for you to be a part of my family's happiness. I just want you to get to know everyone and for them to get to know you." She looked up at him and he looked into her eyes, the big beautiful brown eyes. She put her lips on his and he couldn't fight back. "Okay fine. Let's get this over with". Her family was in the main living room waiting for them to begin practice.

"Hey guys. Look who I finally brought for practice." Nisha grabbed his hands and pulled him into the living room. Pooja and Arjun stood up to greet him.

"Hey Alex! Thank you so much for doing this for us." Pooja was first to come and give him a hug and kiss his cheek. Then they all gave him a hug one at a time. He knew this was a bad idea, but Nisha wouldn't listen to anything he had to say. She insisted he be a part of the wedding. He didn't want to be a part of anything, especially anything that involved putting her in danger.

"Alright so shall we start?" asked Priya once everyone was done greeting each other. She began by giving everyone a spot to stand at. "Guys I have a surprise for you all!" She was excited. "I want to introduce everyone to Nandani, The choreographer!" A woman walked in wearing black tights and a tank top.

"Hi everybody! I'm Nandani and I will help make Priya and Arjun's day even more special with a wonderful dance number. Everyone is assigned a partner, so go ahead and stand shoulder to shoulder with your partner and we will start." She played music and showed everyone a few steps at a time. Alex was cautious with Nisha so close to him. He never danced before today, and he had no intention of dancing after this. He listened to every instruction closely and did exactly as she asked, while staying away from Nisha as far as possible.

"Alright, now grab the girl's hand and twirl her towards you. Then repeat the step together."

Nisha held is hand and came spinning towards him. He didn't know how to stop her. She collided into him and her head hit his elbow. "OW!" she stopped. He tried to back up, but stepped on her feet. "Alex! Are you trying to kill me?!" She was rubbing her head and bending down towards her feet.

"What? No I didn't mean to! I told you I can't do this stuff." He walked out of the room.

He had to get away from them. He walked around towards the backyard and looked out at the view.

"Alex! Alex!" Nisha came after him. She just wouldn't leave him alone. Why does she always make him do crazy things he doesn't want to be involved in?

"Alex what happened? Why did you leave like that? We are all waiting for you. Come back inside please."

"Listen. I told you I can't. Just dance with someone else, I'm not dancing!" He turned away from her and continued to look towards the water. She stood in silence waiting for him to talk to her.

"Alex I'm sorry I didn't know it bothered you so much. I'm sorry." She touched his shoulder.

"I'm going home." He walked back into the house and left.

****

She insisted on walking with him to the subway. It was late and the streets were quiet, except for the usual police sires. They walked hand in hand as she told him about her dream to be an actress.

"you think I can do it?" she asked him.

"Yea, you would be a great actress."

"Well, you're the only one who thinks that. Everyone else thinks I should be a doctor, lawyer, or engineer. Do you see me as an Engineer? Really? No. My mother thinks I'm throwing away my mind by not following Priya's footsteps."

"do what you want. Be who you want. Don't let anyone stop you from being You."

"Where do you come up with this stuff Alex?"

"What stuff??" he was confused. She giggled.

"Good stuff." She kissed him. "stuff that makes me love you more and more every time."

He smiled, "so it's the same stuff, huh?"

"What?"

"the stuff that I love you for." He kissed her. For a few minutes the world froze around them. No one was between them. Nothing interrupted them. For the first time they could just me Alex and Nisha. He wanted to hold her, the essence of her forever. Never let go of the "good stuff".

"You have to get home." He said pulling away from her, "your parents will be worried. I will go down by myself." She kissed him one last time.

"Okay fine. Go." She watched him walk away. He walked backwards watching her and waving at her as he got closer to the station entrance.

He smiled thinking about her as he waited for the train. She made him feel as if everything is going to be good. He is good and nothing is wrong with him. He walked towards the empty benches passing by a homeless man. He wondered if now its all turning out to be fine.

"Hey! You!" He turned around to find the homeless man pointing a knife at him.

"Give me your wallet!"

"I don't have any money!"

"Give it Now! All of it! I'm gonna kill you!"

"Where did this guy come from?" he thought to himself. The guy kept coming at him. He kicked him down and ran back to her.

Nisha! Nisha wait! Nisha!"

She was still walking when she heard her name. She froze in her footstep, it was Alex.

"Nisha!" she turned around and Alex was running towards her with panic in his eyes.

"Alex what happened?! What happened? Tell me! Alex!"

"the guy, he tried to rob me! He is chasing me!" he looked terrified, he didn't want the man to hurt Nisha. They had to get way.

"What guy Alex? What Guy?" She didn't see anyone. She didn't understand what he was talking about.

Alex turned around and saw the man running up the station steps. He had to get her away from here, away from the man.

"He is coming! Let's go! Nisha please let's go from here!" Alex saw the man getting closer.

"Alex, I'm scared, what guy?" she didn't see anyone on the street, "who would be out this late?" she thought to herself as she tried to figure out what was going on with Alex.

"THAT GUY! COMING UP THE STEPS! You see him right? You see him Nisha? I'm not making it up! The guy is coming, we have to leave now! You see him?"

She looked towards the subway. No one was there. No one was coming up the steps. No one was chasing him. She turned to him, fear was surrounding him. She saw how desperate and scared he was about this man chasing him. She put her hand on his cheek. She realized she had to do something to save him.

"I see him Alex. I see the guy."

"Lets go somewhere, away from here! Now Nisha!" he grabbed her hand and they ran to the nearest cabbie.

"Are you okay?" she asked once the cab was moving. "Yea. He was going to kill me and you. Are you okay? I'm glad we got away. He was so close."

She nodded her head, laid her head on his shoulder, and put her hands in his, "he's gone, don't worry now." They didn't talk the rest of the way to her home. When the cab stopped in front of her home she got out, "I'll call you later Alex." She walked up the steps and went in to her home. He watched her go inside and then the cab took him home.

****

"Nisha! Nisha!" Her mother's voice could be piercing sometimes. It was so early in the morning why could she possibly need her at this very moment. She rolled out to the corner of the bed and sat up. She grabbed the band on her side table and put her hair in a bun. She walked down to the dining room where her mother was sitting with a mug of coffee and the mail. When she saw Nisha walk in she jumped out of her chair and ran to her. "It's for You! Take it!" Nisha took the phone and put it to her ear. "Hello" she said calmly not knowing who was on the other side. "Hello Nisha, I'm calling from Universal Studios and we would like to inform you that we loved your audition video and want you to come out to Hollywood for an interview for our upcoming movie." The man on the phone gave her the details of the trip, what she would need to prepare for the interview, and if she passes the interview she will be in the movie. She was no longer drowsy or tired she was shocked. The moment she had been waiting for all these years was happening now! She was going to be in a movie! "Aright I'll talk to you soon, thank you so much! Bye" She jumped up and down in excitement hugging her mother so tightly while they both laughed "OH MY GOD MAA OH MY GOD!! IT HAPPENED FINALLY!!" Priya walked in after hearing the commotion, "what happened?" Nisha grinned from side to side "They Called Me for an INTERVIEW!"

"They asked you to come and interview? You aren't in the movie yet. Relax" Priya went to the counter to get coffee. Nisha stopped jumping and let go of her mother "You are such a negative person Priya! They said if the interview goes well I will be in the movie!!" she walked out of the room and went back upstairs to her room, she had to call Alex.

****

Alex crossed the room, his bare feet shockingly cold against the tile floors. He abruptly stopped in the middle of the room, looked down and smiled. It etched into his face, tugging on both sides of thin, chapped lips. It was for a brief second and then it was gone, only to be replaced by a frown. His eyebrows furrowed together as he bent down to pick up chess board. If was folded in half, looking far too small in his big hands. And then like a shockwave, Alex thought about her. The only light in his dark life; Nisha.

He thought about how her dark rose lips pouted when she wanted something, or how her eyes widened slightly when she was happy. Alex remembered the promise he reluctantly made an hour ago to her. The one promising that he would dance with her, his arms placed firmly against her hips leading her away into the midst of music. Without realizing it, his calloused fingers opened up the chess board. His cool blue eyes shot down, and that was when he let his subconscious consume him.

The dance floor opened up, the black and white tiles sparring across in a vast length. People hovered down from the air, looking as if they were angels descending from the sky. They landed lightly and started to sway to the music. The tight ball gowns were worn by the women, coats and ties by the men, all of whom didn't have a face. They danced as if they were flying, floating seamlessly with each step. Alex turned around to take it all in when he saw someone; a person with a face. It couldn't be. It was Nesha.

Her beauty struck him hard, his heart pounded in his chest; it was like a mallet repeatedly beating against a brass gong. Her long, thick hair was curled into waves, her dark eyes lighting up as she gazed at him. Her dress overflowed onto the floor. With grace she took three easy steps towards Alex. She placed her hand firmly against his shoulder, while grabbing his other hand with her own. With hesitation, Alex gently placed his free hand against her hips.

Soon the music consumed him, the violin drumming into his ears. It was much too loud, but looking into Nesha's eyes, she was all that matter. She started to take a step and he followed. Soon she was moving in an easy rhythm, a pace which Alex could follow. But then she started to go to fast, and Alex couldn't hold on. His grip faltered and Nisha started to move away from him. She moved through the crowd while Alex stood there standing, yearning for her. He took a step forward in attempt to catch her, but his legs failed him and he fell to the floor.

He could feel a weakness consume him as he laid there on the black and white tiles. In this moment he realized he couldn't be the man Nisha wanted. It was too much. He curled onto his side, his knees touching his chest, his heart seizing in time.

Alex looked down to see the chess board thrown aside, and himself sprawled on the floor. His breathing was uneven as he desperately gasped for air. He clutched his stomach and closed his eyes. All he could see was Nisha. He wanted to reach out to her, to touch her, to hold her, to dance with her. But he had just tried hadn't he? And what happened? He had failed, and she had left him broken on the black and white surface; that was all he was worth. After all, Alex didn't see the world as black or white like the chess board, he looked at it as grey, shades of grey.

****

He rang the doorbell and waited for the door to open. It was Nisha. "You came! Come in I just started packing." She grabbed his hand and took him to her room. Her parents had been out of town for Pooja's wedding preparations. As they walked into her room he saw the suitcases spread out around her room and the reality was starting to creep into his mind.

She went straight to the bag on her bed and started putting folded clothes into the suitcase, inspecting each piece to make sure it was properly folded. "I still can't believe this is happening! I finally got a break I've been waiting for. It's so exciting!" She looked ecstatic.

"Nisha, don't go." He had been waiting to tell her this for weeks. He didn't want to ruin her excitement but the simple thought of her leaving him forced him to say it. She laughed at his remark. "Aw Alex I wish I could take you with me. Only I don't even know if I will have to stay longer. Don't worry I will come back." She continued putting clothes in her bag.

He had to stop her from leaving, "Please Nisha don't leave me." He stepped closer to her so he could stop her from packing. She looked up at him in confusion, "are you serious?"

"Yea. Don't leave me." They stood in silence. Abruptly she pushed him away.

"What do you mean don't leave you? I'm not leaving you, I'm going to work. I will be back. This is something I've wanted to do my whole life. You know it's important to me! How can you ask me not to go? Don't you want me to be successful, to be an actress? You were the one who told me you knew I could do it!" She looked furious and he didn't want her to be angry with him, "I want you to be an actress but you don't have to go somewhere else for that." He tried to get closer to her, but she walked away from the bed. She stood in the middle of the room looking out the window for a while. He didn't know what to do to make this better. He couldn't lose her no matter what.

She turned towards him, "I don't get it. My dream is finally coming true and you are telling me that I should wait until it is not out of town. What if that never happens? You are selfish Alex for even asking me to give up on my dreams." Her eyes were different now. No anger, no frustration, no confusion. Alex realized what he saw, sadness in her eyes.

****

"Oh God, Oh God, Oh God!" was all that was going through her mind from the terminal to baggage. She hadn't seen Alex in 5 months, but something had been bothering her ever since she decided to come back. The last time they met wasn't exactly the meeting she had hoped for. Hopefully, she could see him now and fix everything.

She dug in her bag to find her phone. She had it in her bag somewhere. She took it out, "What The Hell!" people in the waiting area turned to look at her. How could her phone be dead! How could this happen. She walked to the nearest pay phone. "Who uses a pay phone anymore?" she thought to herself as she pulled out her wallet. She tried to find change, but she didn't have any quarters. The day she needed a quarter, she couldn't find one. She went back to her luggage. Right in the middle of the lobby Nisha opened her bags to find where she put her charger. She didn't find it in her bags. Could she have left it at the hotel? Well she needed to make this call no matter what.

Who could she ask to lend a quarter? How cheap would that look? She kept walking to the end of the terminal towards the exit. Whatever she had to tell Alex would have to wait until she got home to charge the phone. For now, she was just praying that Raj would be on time. She had called him the night before to discuss the travel information. Maybe Raj could take her to Alex's home?

> I need some time away from you. There is so much going on right now I can't deal with everything. I just wanted to tell you that I accepted the contract for 5 months, and I'm leaving tomorrow. I have to go and please don't stop me. I love you Alex, but I can't keep protecting you from everyone.

> I love you Alex, but I can't keep protecting you from everyone.

He never asked for her protection. He never asked for her love. She came into his life made his life amazing, and then walked out of his life. Now, nothing was the same, everything was a blur and he couldn't find anything worth the frustration of seeing clearly. The waves were higher today on the dock; the water was crashing up and taking everything with it. He paced back and forth on the edge of the dock, remembering the last moments with Nisha.

I can't keep protecting you from everyone.

He was going to see her again today after five months. He was dressed perfectly. he had cut his hair for her. He had shaved his beard for her. He even mustered up the courage to buy the clothes she had picked and dressed accordingly, for her. He had been waiting all morning for her. Now he couldn't remember why he did all this for her. The water was darker and he could see a faded reflection of someone that looked like him, but he couldn't find himself.

I can't keep protecting you from everyone.

The words kept burning in his thoughts as he continued to pace back and forth.

"Nisha! Welcome Back Baby!" Raj came up and hugged her so tight she could barely breathe.

"Get off of me! And grab my luggage, I have to see Alex. "He looked at her with curiosity, but picked up the bags anyway. She went straight out the door without even looking at him. She saw his car parked right outside and walked to it. "Can you please unlock the door?!" He took out the keys and unlocked the car before she could break the window.

As they sat in the car Raj asked her about the trip and how the shooting went. "Honestly Raj, I really am in no mood to talk about that right now. Can you just drive and focus please? Oh and stop at Alex's place before you take me home. I need to see him first." Raj turned to her with somewhat of shock and irritation, "Nisha, the guy can wait. You should see your family first; they have been waiting for you for the last week. By the way if he wanted to see you, wouldn't he have come to the airport? You know I told him you were coming back last night after you called me."

Nisha stared at him with eyes wide open. "You told him? What did he say? Did you tell him the right information? He didn't want to come? Did he look excited?"

"Calm down Nisha. He just said okay. That's it; you know that guy is of few words anyway."

"Oh... so you told him. He still didn't come. Well I don't care. Take me to his apartment or don't bother taking me home."

Raj drove quietly after that. Nisha kept wondering why he didn't come if he knew. Was he that upset with her? Finally the car stopped in front of Alex's building. She literally jumped out of the car. Raj stayed where he was. He obviously had no interest in meeting the guy.

She ran up to the apartment, tripping on the stairs because of her heels. When she got to the door she knocked as loud and she could without disturbing the neighbors. He didn't open the door. "Alex! It's me! Nisha! Alex I'm sorry! Alex open the door!" She kept knocking. Suddenly a lady came out from across the hall.

"Alex not home. Who are you?"

"I'm a friend. Do you know where he is? Did he say anything to you about where he is going?"

"I don't know. He just not home." She slammed the door shut.

Why is he not home at this hour of the day? She had never been this anxious to see anyone in her life, not even her parents. The longer it took to find him, the more difficult it became for her to breathe. She felt it inside of her that something wasn't right. Anxiety was overwhelming her whole body and she couldn't think of anyone else but Alex.

What was the point in waiting for her anyway? He knew she was coming to leave again. He knew she didn't really love him. He wasn't worthy of her love. She simply wanted him to feel loved and important until she got tired of him.

> You know Alex, Nisha only thinks of you as her charity project. She spent time with you, because she felt like she had to. She thought you had no friends, so she had to be your friend. Now, she has better things to focus on.

He kept pacing back and forth at the edge of the dock, struggling to find a reason to stay. A reason to breathe. He felt his chest constrict. He could taste the water filling up his lungs. He took a deep breath to shake the feeling of drowning. The sun started to set deeper into the sky and the windows in the buildings across the harbor began to light up a few at a time. He was like the sun, and the time had come for him to set. After all, no one really needed him now. Not even the one who he wanted to need him. He stared at the water again. Watching the waves once again move with ease yet with so much power. Gradually Alex stopped. He turned facing the water. He knew he couldn't delay anymore. He stood in silence listening to the birds flocking on the harbor. He listened for the last of the boats to pull up to their docks. He watched the rays of sunlight glimmer against the darkness of the water.

I love you Alex.

"Start the car!" Nisha slammed the door of the car and starred at Raj.

"Okay. What happened? What did he say?" Raj started the ignition and headed towards Nisha's home. "Nothing happened. He wasn't there. " she looked frazzled and a bit frightened. Raj knew this wasn't the time to ask Nisha to be sensible or to think about her actions.

She couldn't get rid of the feeling that he was in trouble. "Raj, last night when you told Alex I was coming, how did he behave?" she had to figure out where he disappeared to.

"Huh. Actually I don't know. He looked okay to me." He continued to drive, not even looking at her. Something was conspicuous about the way Raj answered her.

"Raj, why was Alex talking you? Where did you tell him? Did he come to my house?" she had to find out what happened. Raj was hiding something and she could see it in his expression. He was avoiding eye contact and speaking to her. "Raj tell me. What happened?"

"Listen Nisha. I told that guy what he needed to hear. He is always give you stress. He isn't good for anything, but depression. Every time you are around him, you become this different person. None of us like you around him." What was Raj saying. He didn't know Alex. He didn't know anything. "You told him what he need to hear? What was that exactly?" she could feel her blood rising. Who the hell did he think he was?

"I told him that he didn't need to come around your house anymore. He came last night to talk to you. I let him know that he couldn't come whenever he wanted. Then I told him that you were coming today and you already knew what you wanted with your life, so he should understand."

"RAJ! Are you fucking out of your mind?! Stop the car! Stop the damn car!" she reached over to grab the wheel and he braked the car and swerved to the side of the road. She opened the door and got out. "Nisha get in the car. Don't be ridiculous." She turned around. Her anger was visible in her eyes. They were big and intense with frustration. She could kill Raj right now.

"Don't tell me what to do. Leave me alone!" she started to walk away from him. He grabbed her arm and pulled her towards the car. "Stop being crazy Nisha. This is what I'm talking about! He makes you crazy! You do things you don't do without him. He is not for you Nisha! You should stay away from him!" She yanked her arm away from him. "Stop telling me what to do! You don't need to tell me who I should or should be with. How could you do this Raj? You were my best friend. We grew up together. You deceived me." She began to cry. Her anger had overcome her and she couldn't hold it in anymore. She sat on the curb and cried. Her eyes turned red from the tears. She couldn't believe what was happening. She couldn't find Alex. She couldn't tell him how she feels. She couldn't do anything for him.

He never belonged to anyone. He was alone. His father left him alone when he was born. His mother never let him feel like he was her. He wandered through life alone, always yearning for someone to know he exists. Waiting for someone to see him through the barrier he kept around him. He longed for someone to make him feel needed. Nisha had started to help him feel loved and wanted. Then she left. Just like everyone else. She left him alone.

"Hi, I'm Nisha." He saw her captivating smile the first time he saw her.

"Thanks Alex." He could smell the aroma of her perfume from the night of the party.

"I Love you." The touch of her soft skin on his that first night she spent with him.

"I can't keep protecting you from everyone" the sadness in her eyes the last time he saw her.

He stepped off the dock. The feeling of drowning had overcome him. Finally, he wanted to drown, he wanted to blend with the darkness of the water. The cold water shocked his body as he sank slowly down deeper into the depths of the water. His hands started to rise up over his body and he could see the last glimpses of the dock. He began to daze from reality as the suffocating from the lack of air compassed his lungs. He opened his eyes and the suffocation was too much for him.

He tried to grab the phone. He couldn't do anything now. She didn't need him now. He didn't need her.

"Here call him." Raj handed her the phone. "He has to pick up eventually." She wiped her face and dialed Alex's number again. It went to voicemail, "Alex its Nisha. Please pick up your phone, I have been looking for you ever since I got back. Please talk to me. Okay bye." She redialed and held the phone to her ear listening to the ringtone. She had to hear his voice, just once; she had to know he was safe. Voicemail again. She threw the phone against the road and watched it shatter to pieces. She cried once more. She felt devastated. A part of her had been ripped apart from her. She couldn't figure out why she was being so emotional, but she kept crying. The tears kept rolling down her face and she couldn't find a way to stop. She knew it was too late. She knew she would probably never see Alex again.

****

CPSIA information can be obtained
at www.ICGtesting.com
Printed in the USA
BVHW030724070619
550351BV00024B/129/P